This book belongs to:

....

For M and M

A TEMPLAR BOOK

First published in the UK in 2019 by Templar Books,
an imprint of Bonnier Books UK,
The Plaza, 535 King's Road, London, SW10 0SZ
www.templarco.co.uk
www.bonnierbooks.co.uk

Copyright © 2019 by Templar Books

1 3 5 7 9 10 8 6 4 2

ISBN 978-1-78741-504-1 (Hardback)
ISBN 978-1-78741-516-4 (Paperback)

This book was typeset in Times New Roman
The illustrations were created with pen and ink and watercolour

Edited by Alison Ritchie
Designed by Genevieve Webster
Production Controller Nick Read

Printed in China

Sam Usher

FREE

templar
books

When I woke up
this morning,
one of the birds
was poorly.

I said, "Grandad,
we have to do something!"

So we made him a cosy bed and
Grandad found his book of bird facts.

We gave him a drink of water and Grandad said,
"Look! He's getting better already.
Let's put him back in the garden."

I said, "Oh, do we have to?"

And Grandad said,
"Yes I think so.
He won't want to be
cooped up in here."

So we put him
back outside,
and we thought,
that's that.

It was time for breakfast so we weighed the flour,

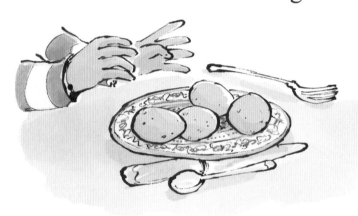

poured the milk, cracked the eggs, mixed it up . . .

. . . and flipped the pancakes.

And I said, "Grandad!
Look who it is!"

"Maybe he's hungry.
Can we give him some of our pancakes?"

And Grandad said, "Let's see if he likes
berries instead."

So we put him by
the blackberry bush,
and we thought,
that's that.

When it was time for lunch
we sliced some bread,

found the fillings . . .

. . . and made triple-deckers.

And I said, "Grandad! Look who it is!"

"Do you think he might be lonely?"

And Grandad said, "He might be. Let's take him outside
in case any of his friends show up."

So we put him
by the birdbath,
and we thought,
that's that.

At teatime, we chose
our favourite cups,

boiled the kettle,

filled the teapot

and found the biscuits.

And I said, "Grandad!
Look who it is!
I think he likes us,
he keeps coming back."

We spent the rest of the afternoon together.

And I said,
"Grandad, please can he stay forever?"

But Grandad said,
"I think he'll be happier if he's free.
Look, we need to find a tree like this and
help him find his way home."

So we gathered our expedition equipment . . .

. . . and I said, "Look, Grandad, there's the tree,
right at the top of that mountain!"

It was a long
way away . . .

. . . but we made it!

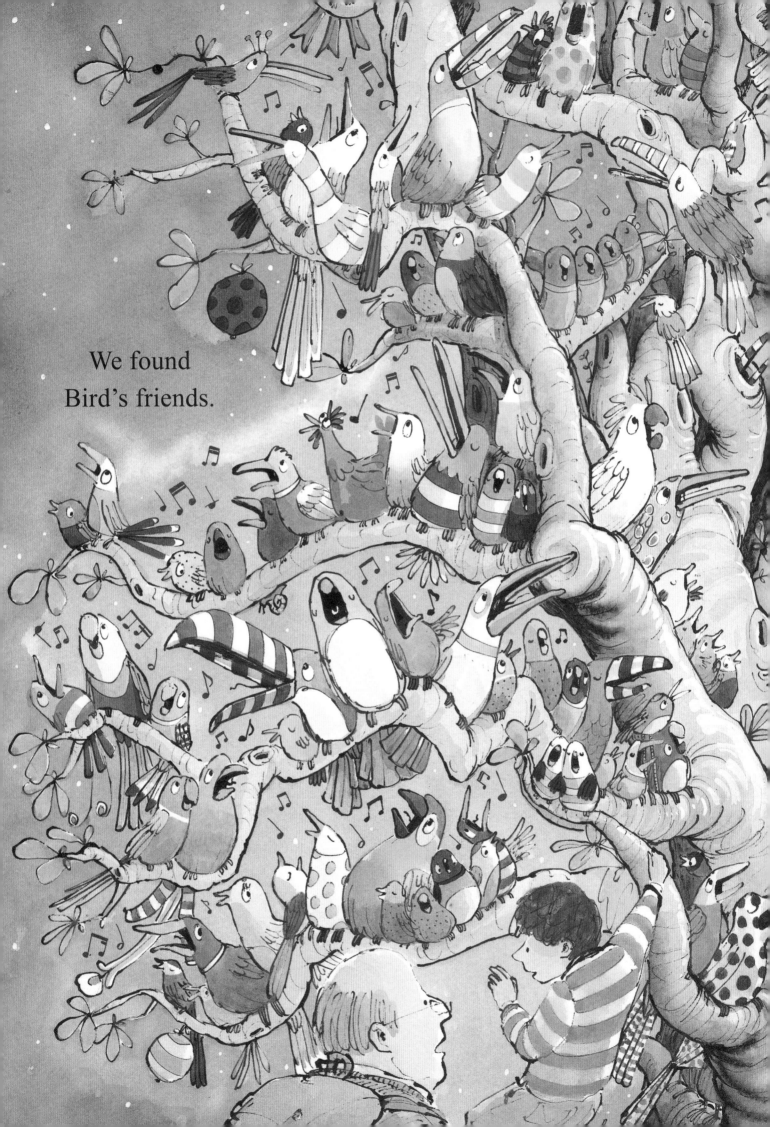

We found
Bird's friends.

Boiling point

Water normally boils at 100°C, which is called its boiling point. At this temperature it will cook an egg and make a cup of tea. But the boiling point is not fixed. Water under pressure can get much hotter before it starts to boil. That is how pressure cookers work. Inside, water reaches 120°C before it starts to boil and the food cooks faster. Pressure squeezes the water so that steam bubbles cannot form. Even outside a pressure cooker, pressure from the atmosphere is trying to stop bubbles forming. In space or in a vacuum, where there is no pressure, water will boil from the heat of your hand.

Steam power

When water is heated so that it turns to steam, it expands enormously. The steam can be used in an engine to drive it along. As the steam expands it pushes pistons in and out, and these make the wheels go round.

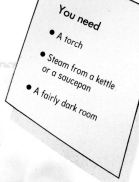

You need
• A torch
• Steam from a kettle or a saucepan
• A fairly dark room

Water experiment

SPOT THE WATER DROPLETS!

Warning!
You must be very careful when doing this experiment because steam can be hot! Ask an adult to help you.

Shine the torch towards you from behind the steam. As the steam drifts up you should be able to see the tiny water droplets.

Mixing

Some solids, such as sugar or salt, mix with water completely. This is called **dissolving**, and the mixture is called a **solution**. However long you leave a sugar solution, the sugar will not separate from the water – unless, of course, the water evaporates. Clay and mud do not dissolve. If you mix them with water and then leave the mixture to stand, the clay and mud fall to the bottom in a layer of **sediment**.

Mud mixed with water in the Tana River, Kenya.

Liquid layers

Oil and water do not mix. Oil floats in a layer on top of water. If you shake them together, both may break up into round drops called **globules**. The oil globules float to the surface of the water where they join up with each other again. You can see water globules in the oil layer in the picture.

If you shake oil and water together very hard, the globules become tiny and do not join together. Oil and water mixed in this way is called an **emulsion**.

Water experiment

MAKE AN EMULSION!

1 Fill the bottle a quarter full with water.

2 Add the same amount of cooking oil.

3 Screw the cap tightly on the bottle. Shake the bottle hard up and down.

The oil and water form a mixture called an emulsion. If you leave the emulsion standing, it will gradually separate into oil and water. Try adding a drop of detergent and then shaking the bottle again. The emulsion separates much more slowly now.

You need

- A medium-sized empty medicine bottle with a tightly fitting cap
- Cooking oil
- Water

Three droppers, each with a different coloured ink, are squeezed into a tank of water.

The drops of ink are heavier than water and sink. As they sink they stir up the water, which breaks them up.

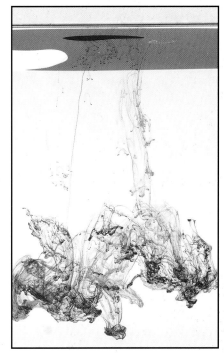

The broken drops stir up more water, which makes them spread in all directions. This is how rain mixes with pond water.

Flowing

Water flows down mountainsides in rivers and waterfalls, and flows out of a jug when you pour it. It also flows out of taps into your bath. **Gravity** is the force on Earth that pulls everything downwards. Gravity makes water flow.

When you stand by a big waterfall you can get an idea of the enormous power of falling water. It pours down, thundering and pounding all day and night. As it flows down mountains it wears away the rocks, making valleys. It grinds rocks into smooth pebbles. And it carries away tonnes and tonnes of **silt** – finely ground rocks and sand.

Water work

Fast streams and rivers take many thousands of years to carve deep valleys. Trees and plants hold the soil together with their roots and stop it being washed away. When people cut down trees and let sheep and goats eat all the grass, soil that has taken hundreds of years to form can be washed away in one heavy storm.

Water squirts from this frog in a jet that is pulled downwards by gravity.

You need
- A round plastic carton lid
- A drinking straw
- Scissors
- A steel skewer or a thin knitting needle

Water experiment

WATER WHEELIES!

1 Cut a 7cm section from the drinking straw.

2 Cut slits round the edge of the plastic lid. Make a hole in the centre and push the straw through.

3 Bend the cut sections over, all at the same angle. Push the skewer through the straw. Hold the water wheel under a gently running tap and it will whizz round!

Water power

Streams and rivers rushing down mountains have lots of energy. If the water can be made to drive a wheel, the energy can be used to do work such as making electricity. The water can be trapped and stored in huge dams. Water is let out of the dams at a steady rate to drive electricity generators.

The energy in this flowing stream turns the wheel which drives machinery in the mill.

The Hoover Dam on the Colorado River, USA, can generate over 1,300 megawatts of electric power.

Spinning

When water is spun around, it moves away from the centre towards the outside. You can see this if you take a stick and stir water in a bucket. The water starts to climb up the sides of the bucket, leaving a dip in the centre. Water sometimes behaves like this naturally in fast rivers, making **whirlpools**. There are sometimes whirlpools in the sea, where strong currents flow between islands. Small boats can be tossed about and sunk if they get trapped in a big whirlpool.

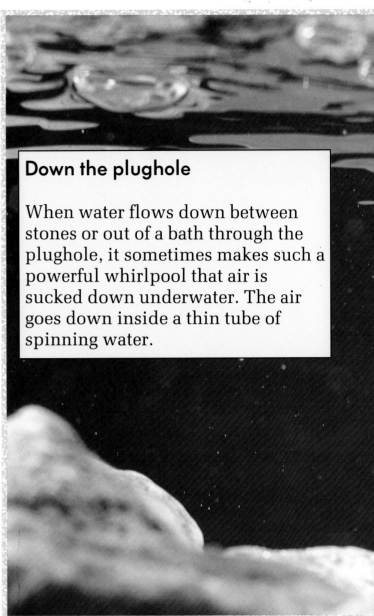

Down the plughole

When water flows down between stones or out of a bath through the plughole, it sometimes makes such a powerful whirlpool that air is sucked down underwater. The air goes down inside a thin tube of spinning water.

Most water spouts are about 8 metres across and around 100 metres high.

Water spout

A whirlwind is air that is spinning very fast. Whirlwinds over land suck up dust and sand. Over the sea they suck up water into water spouts. It is said that little fish are sometimes sucked up with the water and come down in salty rain – but this is probably just a tall story.

A small whirlpool in a stream sucks air down in a tube of spinning water.

Sprinkler

When water squirts from a garden sprinkler, the force of the water jets sends the sprinkler whirling round. As the water spins round, the drops fly away from the centre.

Did you know?

If you stir up sand in a jar of water, it will settle in a pyramid at the bottom.

Water experiment

GLUG OR NO GLUG?

1 Fill both bottles with water.

2 On the word "go", get your friend to empty one bottle while you empty yours.

3 If you hold your bottle upside down and swirl it around, a whirlpool will form inside it and it will empty much more quickly than your friend's.

You need
- Two bottles
- A friend

19

Surface

Some insects can walk on the surface of water. This is because water has a very thin stretchy skin on the surface. The skin forms because water is made up of tiny parts, called **molecules**, that are attracted to each other. Water molecules at the surface are more attracted to the water molecules below them than they are to the air, so they get pulled down slightly. This is  called **surface tension**. As a result, a stretchy skin is formed. It is surface tension that makes drops of water form into round shapes and holds a jet of water together.

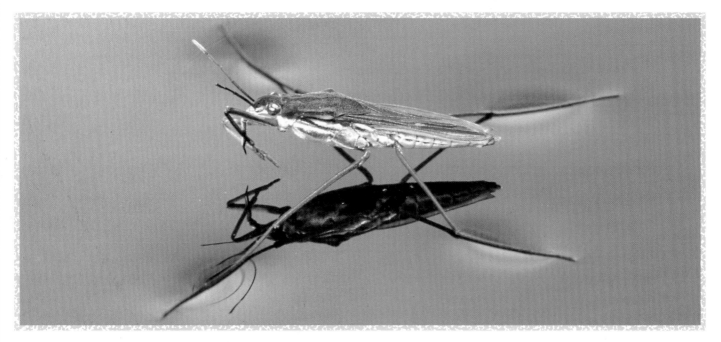

Surface dwellers

This pond skater is making dimples in the water where its feet press down on the pond's surface layer.

When streams become polluted with detergent, this layer is changed and surface dwelling insects can no longer live there.

Breaking the surface

Wind makes waves on the surface of the sea. Big waves travel for hundreds of kilometres across the ocean. When they reach shallow water near land, they are slowed at the bottom but keep going at the top, so they just fall over.

Water experiment

SKIMMING BEADS!

1 Fill the washing-up bowl with water and stir in a few drops of detergent without making too many bubbles.

2 Dip some water out of the bowl with the jug. Pour water gently over the back of a spoon, holding it about 1cm above the surface of the water.

Drips from the spoon form shining beads which glide over the surface. These are not bubbles.

You need
- A plastic washing-up bowl
- A jug
- Washing-up liquid
- A spoon

Water beads

You can sometimes see shiny beads of water skating over the surface of a stream near a waterfall.

These beads are formed by surface tension. Each one lasts for only a second or two.

21

Soaking up

If you dip one corner of a sponge into water and leave it there, the whole sponge will gradually become sodden. This is because sponges are full of tiny holes which draw the water up. But what makes water soak into the holes in this way?

To understand this, you have to know what a **capillary** is. A capillary is a very thin tube. When the end of a capillary is put into water, the water is pulled up inside the tube. The tiny holes in a sponge are capillaries, so water gets drawn into them until the sponge  is full. Water soaks into blotting paper because the gaps between the paper **fibres** act as capillaries.

Capillary tubes

Thin glass tubes arranged in order of size have been dipped into coloured water. The pull of surface tension makes water rise in the tubes. It rises highest in the thinnest tube because this contains the least weight of water. If you look closely at the surface of the water in the tubes, you will see it is not flat but curved, like a saucer.

Put a stick of celery into a jar of water containing a few drops of red food dye. Leave it for a few hours.

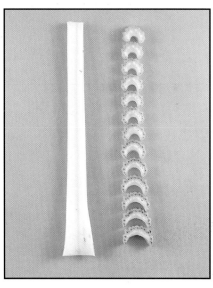

If you cut the stalk into several sections, you can see how far the dyed water has been soaked up.

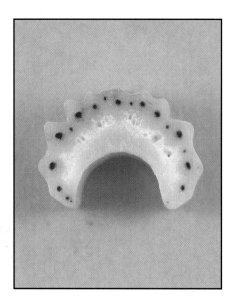

As the dye is soaked up, it colours the dots in the sections red. Each red dot contains about 50 capillaries.

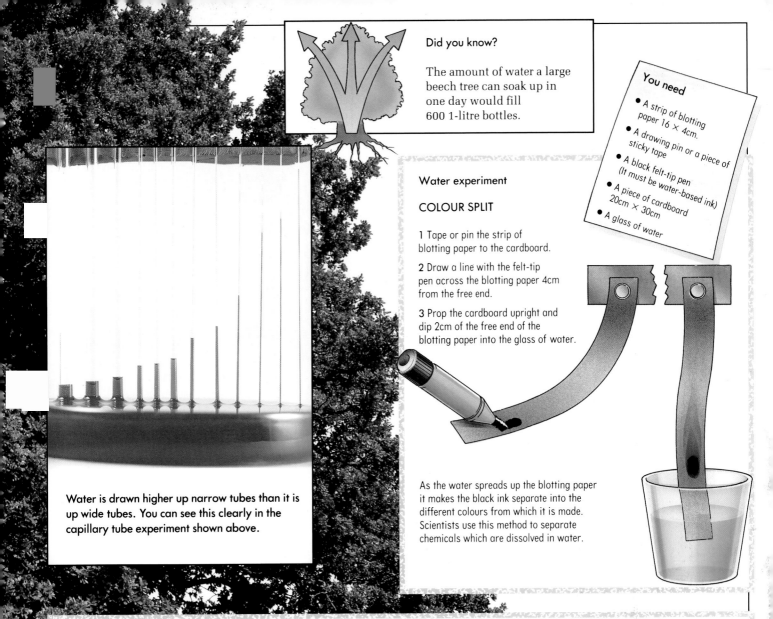

Did you know?

The amount of water a large beech tree can soak up in one day would fill 600 1-litre bottles.

Water experiment

COLOUR SPLIT

1 Tape or pin the strip of blotting paper to the cardboard.

2 Draw a line with the felt-tip pen across the blotting paper 4cm from the free end.

3 Prop the cardboard upright and dip 2cm of the free end of the blotting paper into the glass of water.

As the water spreads up the blotting paper it makes the black ink separate into the different colours from which it is made. Scientists use this method to separate chemicals which are dissolved in water.

Water is drawn higher up narrow tubes than it is up wide tubes. You can see this clearly in the capillary tube experiment shown above.

The wood of a tree, like this oak, contains many capillaries. You can see them as tiny holes.

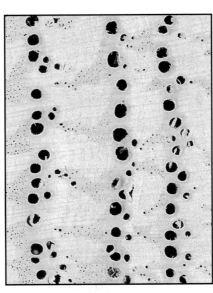

If you look at the holes through a powerful microscope, you will see that they are round tubes.

Thirsty plants

Plants take in water from the soil through their roots. As water evaporates through tiny holes underneath the plant's leaves, more water gets drawn up through the plant's stem or trunk. It is a long way for water to tunnel from the roots of a tree to the leaves at the top. The roots help by 'pushing' water up the trunk.

Floating

Fill a jug with water right to the brim. Hold a cup under the jug's lip to catch any water that spills out and gently float something in the jug, perhaps a small jar. It doesn't matter what you float, it will always push out its own weight in water. This fact was discovered more than 2,000 years ago by Archimedes, a Greek scientist. He discovered it when he sat down in a full bath. He ran into the street shouting "Eureka!" (I have found it).

The Dead Sea is so salty that people can float in it with their arms out of the water.

Air trapped in the ducklings' feathers makes them float more than half out of the water.

How dense can you get?

Imagine a cube of water – like a sugar cube – with each side 1 centimetre long. This is called a **cubic centimetre** (1 cc) of water and weighs exactly 1 gram (1g). If you dissolve salt in 1 cc of water, it weighs more than 1g because the water is denser.

Things float more easily in a dense liquid. The water of the Dead Sea contains so much salt that people can float in it easily. Mercury is a liquid metal that is thirteen times more dense than water. Stones float in it like corks in water.

Water experiment

EGG-STRAORDINARY!

You need
- An egg
- Salt
- A teaspoon
- A glass of water

1 Fill the glass with water and put in the egg, which will sink.

2 Add 3 or 4 teaspoons of salt and stir gently. The egg should then float. If it does not, add more salt.

The egg floats because salt water is more dense than fresh water.

What happens if you gently pour more fresh water over the floating egg?

A light bulb released under the water floats up quickly.

The bulb is very light so it shoots up through the water's surface.

It takes a lot of water with it and makes a big splash.

Drips and drops

Imagine a rain drop falling from a cloud. It starts off tiny and just drifts downwards. As it falls it gets bigger and comes down faster. Surface tension (see pages 20 and 21) is trying to pull it into a perfectly round shape. But as it rushes down through the air, air resistance is trying to flatten it. When the drop grows to about 5mm across, surface tension can't hold it together any more and it breaks into smaller drops. Each of these may then start to grow again. Drips from a tap do not get big enough or fall fast enough for air resistance to break them up.

Spikes

When a small raindrop falls onto a pond it makes a hole in the surface that quickly fills with water. The water tries so hard to fill the hole that it rises up into a spike. Then the spike breaks up into two or three little drops.

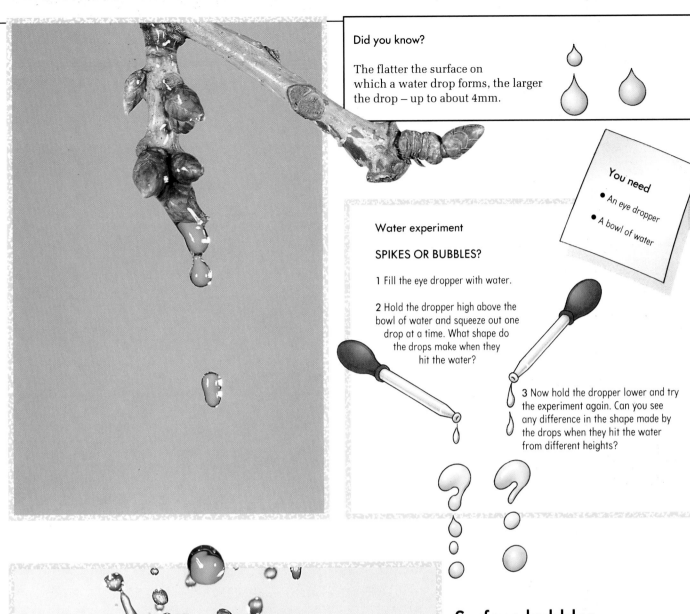

Did you know?

The flatter the surface on which a water drop forms, the larger the drop – up to about 4mm.

You need
- An eye dropper
- A bowl of water

Water experiment

SPIKES OR BUBBLES?

1 Fill the eye dropper with water.

2 Hold the dropper high above the bowl of water and squeeze out one drop at a time. What shape do the drops make when they hit the water?

3 Now hold the dropper lower and try the experiment again. Can you see any difference in the shape made by the drops when they hit the water from different heights?

Surface bubbles

When a large raindrop falls on a pond it makes a big hole in the water. This time there is no spike of water. Instead, a bubble, lasting just a few seconds, appears on the surface. That is because the water has closed over the hole, trapping air beneath the surface. Look out for spikes and bubbles next time you are near a pond or puddle in the rain.

27

Bubbles

Did you know?

Soap bubbles floating in air last longer in damp weather than dry weather.

Bubbles are pockets of gas. They are round for the same reason that raindrops are round, for both are shaped by surface tension (see pages 20 and 21). A bubble rising through water is rather like a falling raindrop. Surface tension inside the bubble tries to keep it a round shape, but water resistance outside pushes it into a flat shape. If a rising bubble is too big, water resistance breaks it up into smaller bubbles. Soap bubbles floating in air are made of a thin skin of water.

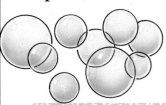

Tadpoles make froth, which is lots of tiny bubbles. The froth lasts because of slime in the water.

Natural gas

Dead leaves at the bottom of a pond sometimes rot and produce marsh gas. This has hydrogen in it and when lit burns with a blue flame. When it burns, oxygen in the air joins with the hydrogen, and guess what it makes – water! (see p.5)

Gas bubbles rushing to a pond's surface from dead leaves.

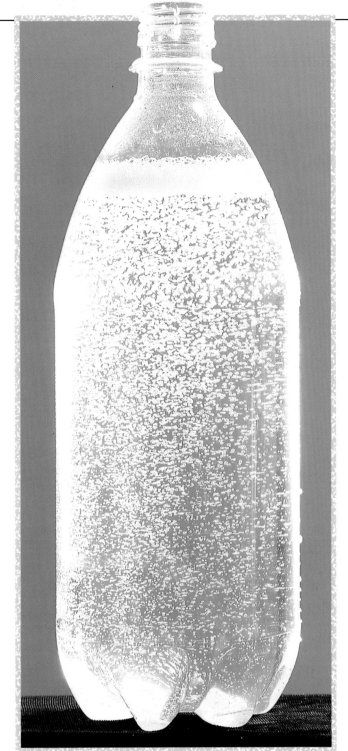

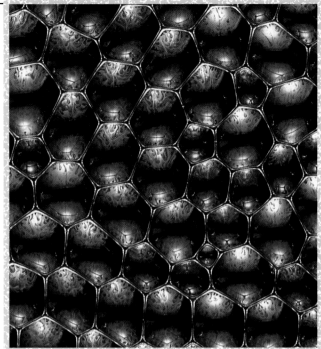

Detergent bubbles squeezed together are no longer round. They may have five or seven sides, but most have six, like honeycomb.

Fizzy pop

Pressure makes gas dissolve. Fizzy drinks are full of dissolved **carbon dioxide** gas. It has been put in under pressure. Opening the bottle releases the pressure, so the gas bubbles out of solution. If you open the top slowly, you can hear it hissing out.

Water experiment

THE AMAZING BOUNCING LENTILS!

1 Fill the jug three-quarters full of water. Add an eggcup of vinegar and two teaspoons of bicarbonate of soda. Gently stir the mixture to get rid of the froth.

2 Drop in a teaspoon of lentils, which will sink. Soon they will start to move – first rising to the surface then sinking again. They will continue to do this for some time.

Gas bubbles form on the lentils. The bubbles make the lentils rise to the surface. At the surface the bubbles burst and the lentils sink to the bottom again.

Warning!
Ask an adult to help you with this experiment.

You need
● A glass jug
● An egg cup
● A teaspoon
● Vinegar
● Bicarbonate of soda
● 6 Lentils

Depth

The deeper you go underwater, the greater the water pressure. Ten kilometres under the ocean the pressure is more than 1 tonne for every square centimetre. Some animals can live there without being squashed because their bodies are made of liquids and solids that cannot be **compressed**. This means they cannot be squeezed smaller. But if you bring these creatures to the surface they swell up as dissolved gases in their bodies form bubbles.

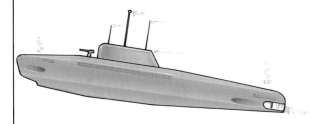

Fish have swim bladders to help them rise or sink in the water.

This angler fish lives in the depths of the ocean. Its body can withstand the great pressure of the water.

30

Did you know?

The deepest ocean descent ever made was 10,917 metres, (6.78 miles). It was made in the American bathyscaphe *Trieste* in 1960 in the Pacific Ocean.

Rising and falling

Divers and submarines rise in the sea by making themselves lighter. To sink, they make themselves heavier. Fish rise and fall using a special air-filled bag inside their bodies called a **swim bladder**. This is filled with air and makes the fish float. To sink, the fish uses its muscles to squeeze air out of the bladder. Air-breathing sea creatures, such as turtles, do not have swim bladders. They have to work hard to swim down from the surface.

Water experiment

A DIVER'S GOTTA LOTTA BOTTLE!

You need
- A pen top
- Plasticine
- An empty plastic 1-litre bottle

1 Weight the bottom of the pen top with a small piece of Plasticine until, when filled with air, it just floats.

2 Fill the bottle to the top with water and carefully float the weighted pen top in it.

3 Screw on the bottle cap tightly. Squeeze the bottle gently and the 'diver' will sink. Release the bottle and then it will rise to the surface.

When you squeeze the bottle, the air bubble inside the pen top is squeezed smaller and can no longer support the weight of the Plasticine. This is why the 'diver' sinks.

The weight of water

The human body cannot survive deep under water without special equipment to protect it from the great pressure. Divers wear thick suits and have air pumped down to them at the same pressure as the water where they are working. For really deep dives, people have to go in submarines made of strong metal with very thick glass windows that can withstand tremendous pressure.

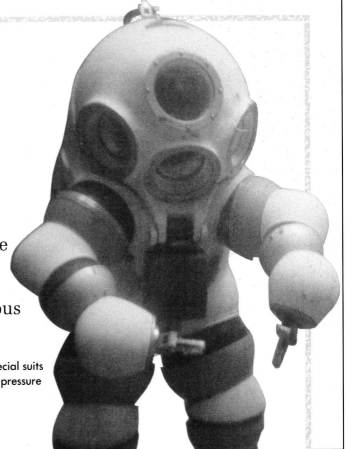

Submarines are built to withstand the tremendous pressure of the deep sea.

Deep-sea divers have special suits to protect them from the pressure of the water.

Water words

Capillary A very thin tube.

Carbon dioxide A gas made of oxygen and carbon. We breathe out carbon dioxide.

Compress To squeeze something and make it smaller.

Condense To change from a vapour to a liquid.

Cubic centimetre A cube with each side 1cm long.

Dissolve To mix completely with a liquid.

Drizzle Very fine rain.

Emulsion A mixture of tiny globules of oil and water.

Evaporate To change from a liquid to vapour.

Fibres Tiny threads.

Geyser A spout of steam and hot water from under the ground.

Glacier A river of ice.

Globule A small round drop of liquid.

Gravity The force that pulls objects back towards Earth.

Hydrogen A gas found in water and in all plants and animals.

Molecule The smallest amount of a chemical substance that can exist by itself. Every water molecule contains two atoms of hydrogen and one atom of oxygen.

Oxygen A gas found in water, the air and all living things. We take in oxygen when we breathe.

Sediment Solid particles that sink to the bottom of a liquid.

Silt Finely ground-up rocks and mud carried along by rivers.

Solution A solid or gas mixed completely with a liquid.

Surface tension A force that pulls the surface of liquids down, making a thin skin on top.

Swim bladder An air-filled bag inside a fish's body that enables it to rise and fall in the water.

Water vapour A mass of tiny drops of water in the air.

Waterproof Having a surface that water cannot pass through.

Whirlpool Water spinning round.

Index

Picture credits

All photographs are by Kim Taylor and Jane Burton except for Zefa title page, 4-5, 17 bottom right, 20-21; Tony Stone 4 bottom left, 24; World Wide 4 inset left; Bruce Coleman 4 inset right, 7, 8 bottom left and right, 10 bottom left, 12, 16-17, 17 bottom left, 22-23 background; Science Photo Library 13, 18; Planet Earth Pictures 30 bottom left and right; Aspect Pictures 31.